my first ★ Bedtime storybook

Disney PRESS

Los Angeles • New York

First Hardcover Edition, April 2019 10 9 8 7 6 5 4 3 2 1
ISBN 978-1-368-03915-4

FAC-025393-19011

Library of Congress Control Number: 2018951304
Printed in China

For more Disney Press fun, visit www.disneybooks.com

Contents

This book belongs to:

_____

CINDERELLA

Once there was a girl called CINDERELLA.

She lived with her wicked stepmother and stepsisters.

One day, they were invited to a royal ball!

Cinderella wanted to wear an old dress that had belonged to her mother. But Cinderella was so busy with her CHORES she had no time to fix it.

Luckily, Cinderella had little bird and mouse friends. They fixed her dress so she could go to the royal ball! But Cinderella's stepsisters were JEALOUS and tore the dress apart.

Heartbroken, Cinderella ran outside to the garden and cried. Suddenly, her FAIRY GODMOTHER appeared! She wanted to help.

She said "Bibbidi-Bobbidi-Boo" and waved her magic wand. Cinderella looked down to find herself dressed in a beautiful gown and a pair of glass slippers. She was ready for the ball. But at the stroke of MIDNIGHT, the spell would break.

At the ball, the Prince asked Cinderella to dance.

They danced together all night and FELL IN LOVE.

Before they knew it, the clock began to strike midnight. The spell was about to be broken! As Cinderella hurried home, she left one GLASS SLIPPER behind.

The Prince decided he would marry the girl whose foot fit the glass slipper. Cinderella's stepsisters tried it on, but their feet were too BIG. Then the slipper accidentally broke!

Luckily, Cinderella had the other glass slipper!

Soon Cinderella and the Prince were married, and they lived HAPPILY EVER AFTER.

Disney
PRINCESS

THE
LITTLE
MERMAID

Ariel was a little mermaid with a beautiful voice. One day, she spotted a man called Prince Eric on board his ship.

Ariel longed to meet the prince, but she knew her father, KING TRITON, would never approve.

Suddenly, storm clouds filled the sky. The prince's ship lurched back and forth, causing Eric to fall overboard!

Ariel RESCUED him and brought him to shore.

Ariel sang to the prince. But when he began to wake up, she dove back into the SEA. As Eric made his way back to the castle, Ariel watched from afar.

Below the waves, URSULA THE SEA WITCH
spied on Ariel. She promised to make Ariel human if
she would just give Ursula her voice. But Eric would
have to kiss Ariel before the third sunset, or the little
mermaid would belong to Ursula!

Ariel agreed and became human. Eric found Ariel on the beach. He asked her if she was the girl who had SUNG TO HIM, but Ariel couldn't speak. So Eric took her to his castle to help her.

The next day, Eric and Ariel spent a wonderful afternoon together. He almost KISSED her, but Ursula's evil eels stopped them.

Ursula disguised herself as a human girl named VANESSA. She carried Ariel's voice in her shell necklace, and with it, she cast a spell on Eric.

Under Ursula's spell, Eric announced that he was going to marry Vanessa the very next day!

At the wedding, Ariel's bird
friend Scuttle discovered the
TRUTH about Vanessa. He
broke the shell necklace,
which gave Ariel her voice
back!

Eric was just about to kiss his TRUE LOVE, Ariel, when the sun set on the third day. It was too late! Ariel became a mermaid again.

Now Ursula ruled Ariel *and* the ocean! Eric jumped on a ship and steered it out to sea to challenge her. After a fierce battle, the sea witch was DESTROYED.

The ocean was safe again, but Ariel and Eric couldn't be together. So King Triton agreed to use his magic to make his daughter human. Eric and Ariel were married and lived HAPPILY EVER AFTER.

Once there was a young princess named RAPUNZEL. Her hair had magical powers. A woman named Mother Gothel wanted this power, so she kidnapped Rapunzel and raised her in a tower.

Every year on her birthday, Rapunzel saw glowing LIGHTS in the sky. They seemed meant for her.

While Mother Gothel was away one day, a thief known as Flynn Rider climbed up the tower with a stolen crown in his bag. When he got to the top, Rapunzel hit him with a FRYING PAN and took the crown away from him!

Rapunzel told Flynn she would give him back
the crown if he took her to see the lights. Leaving the
tower after so many years was scary, but Rapunzel
was EXCITED. She and Flynn traveled for days and
days. Rapunzel learned that Flynn's real name was
EUGENE. By the time they reached the kingdom,
Eugene and Rapunzel had become friends.

As a gift, Eugene gave Rapunzel a FLAG with an emblem of the sun on it.

That night, Rapunzel's DREAMS came true. She saw the beautiful floating lanterns up close! To thank Eugene, Rapunzel decided to give the crown back to him. But he didn't care about it anymore. He only cared for Rapunzel.

Later, Eugene was captured by some bad guys.
Mother Gothel found Rapunzel. She lied and told her
that Eugene had left, so Rapunzel agreed to return
to the tower with her. But as she gazed at the flag,
Rapunzel realized it was familiar. It was the flag of
her kingdom. She was the LOST PRINCESS!

Eugene managed to escape. He climbed up to Rapunzel's tower, but Mother Gothel wounded him!

Rapunzel made a deal. If she could use her hair to HEAL Eugene, she would stay with Mother Gothel forever.

But Eugene wouldn't let her. Before Rapunzel could save him, Eugene reached up and cut off her hair! The magic instantly disappeared, and Mother Gothel turned to DUST.

Thinking all hope of saving Eugene was lost,
Rapunzel cried. But as her tears fell on his face,
he was magically HEALED!

At long last, Rapunzel

was reunited with her parents.

And Princess Rapunzel and Eugene lived

HAPPILY EVER AFTER!

Once upon a time, a woman asked a spoiled prince for shelter. He refused to help her, so she cast a spell on him and everyone in the castle. Unless the Prince could love and earn someone's love in return, he would remain a BEAST FOREVER.

Not far away, in a little village in France, there lived a girl named BELLE. She was different from the other villagers. She lived with her father and she loved reading books.

One day, Belle's father stumbled upon the

BEAST'S CASTLE and was taken prisoner! Belle

went looking for him. When she found her father,

she offered to take his place.

Some enchanted objects in the castle tried to
cheer Belle up by entertaining her. They urged
the Beast to be GENTLE with Belle, but he had
a terrible temper.

When Belle got the chance, she escaped from the castle. But a PACK OF WOLVES found her.

Just in time, the Beast caught up to Belle and fought off the wolves!

From that moment on, Belle saw a different side of the Beast. They began to spend more time together. And soon, the Beast realized he had fallen in LOVE with Belle.

Unfortunately, the VILLAGERS learned that the Beast was holding Belle captive. They rushed to the castle to attack him.

The Beast tried to defend himself, but it was no use. He fell from the roof, badly wounded. Belle rushed to his side.

"I LOVE YOU," Belle whispered, sobbing.

With those three words, the SP€LL was broken!

Belle watched in wonder as the Beast

transformed back into a handsome man.

And they lived HAPPILY EVER AFTER!

Disney
PRINCESS

ALADDIN

At the palace in the kingdom of Agrabah, PRINCESS JASMINE argued with her father, the Sultan. The law said she must marry a prince by her next birthday. But Jasmine did not want to marry a prince. She wanted to marry for LOVE.

Jasmine decided to run away. In the marketplace, she saw a hungry little boy. She took an apple and gave it to the boy. But she had no way to pay for it, so the merchant called her a THIEF!

Suddenly, a boy who lived on the streets appeared. His name was ALADDIN. He helped Jasmine get away from the merchant.

Meanwhile, a greedy man named Jafar wanted to enter the Cave of Wonders. But when he discovered that only a DIAMOND IN THE ROUGH could enter, he grew angry. With a magic spell, he discovered that the Diamond in the Rough was Aladdin.

Jafar sent his men to return the princess home.

Then Jafar offered Aladdin a deal—if he took a **MAGIC LAMP** from the cave, he would be free.

Aladdin agreed.
But when he rubbed
the lamp, a genie
came out!

The Genie
offered Aladdin
THREE WISHES.

Aladdin promised to free the Genie from the lamp
with his last wish.

For his first wish, Aladdin asked the Genie to turn
him into a prince named Ali. Prince Ali took Jasmine
on a MAGIC CARPET RIDE, and they found
themselves falling in love.

But then Jafar's parrot, Iago, stole the magic lamp. Now the Genie had to grant Jafar's wishes! Jafar wished to become the most powerful SORCERER in the world. He held the royals captive.

Jafar's next wish was to become an all-powerful GENIE. But Jafar had forgotten something. Now that he was a genie, he could be trapped in a lamp!

With Jafar gone, Aladdin was able to use his last WISH to free the Genie.

To make his daughter happy, the Sultan decided to change the law. Jasmine could now marry anyone she wanted to! Jasmine chose Aladdin, and together they lived HAPPILY EVER AFTER.

Disney
PRINCESS

SNOW WHITE
AND THE
SEVEN DWARFS

One day, a beautiful girl named SNOW WHITE met a handsome prince. They were drawn to each other right away.

But Snow White's stepmother, the Evil Queen, was JEALOUS of Snow White's beauty and charm. So she commanded a huntsman to get rid of Snow White!

Snow White had to get away from the Evil Queen.
Scared and alone, she ran into the FOREST. She
soon came upon a cottage.

Inside the cottage lived SEVEN DWARFS: Doc, Bashful, Sleepy, Grumpy, Sneezy, Happy, and Dopey. The Dwarfs adored their new friend. She was kind and liked to laugh with them. They asked her to stay with them.

But when the Evil Queen found out that the Huntsman had not gotten rid of Snow White, she was angry. She transformed herself into an old woman and gave Snow White a poisoned apple. As soon as Snow White took a bite, she fell to the floor! Only LOVE'S FIRST KISS could break the spell.

When the Dwarfs saw what had happened to Snow White, they CHASED the Queen. Lightning struck, causing her to fall off a cliff and disappear forever. But still, the spell did not break.

Time passed. Day after day, the Dwarfs kept watch over SNOW WHITE in the forest.

When the Prince finally arrived, the Dwarfs were overjoyed. And with his kiss, Snow White awoke!

Together at last, Snow White and her prince lived HAPPILY EVER AFTER.